Wait! No Paint!

Written and illustrated by
Bruce Whatley

HARPERCOLLINSPUBLISHERS

For Dave, my oldest friend

Wait! No Paint! Copyright © 2001 by Bruce Whatley
Printed in U.S.A. All rights reserved. www.harperchildrens.com
Library of Congress Cataloging-in-Publication Data
Whatley, Bruce.
Wait! No paint! / written and illustrated by Bruce Whatley.
p.   cm.
The three little pigs are in their usual trouble with the big bad wolf, until a mysterious
Voice gets involved and mixes things up.
ISBN 0-06-028270-3—ISBN 0-06-028271-1 (lib. bdg.)
[1. Pigs—Fiction.   2. Wolves—Fiction.   3. Illustrators—Fiction.]   I. Three little pigs.   II. Title.
PZ7.W55553 Wai   2001   [E]—dc21   00-61351
Typography by Al Cetta   1 2 3 4 5 6 7 8 9 10   ❖   First Edition

Once upon a time there were three little pigs. They lived together in an old house on top of a tall hill . . .

along with seventy-three other little pigs.

Which is why they decided to leave home
and build their own little houses.

The first little pig built his house out of straw.

The second little pig built his house out of sticks.

The third little pig built his house out of bricks.
Bricks would keep out the wind, the rain, and
the big, bad wolf.

The first little pig had just finished building his house when he heard a splash.

"Oops!" said a Voice from nowhere in particular. "I spilt my juice."

"Yuck!" said the first little pig. Now his new straw house was soggy and sticky.

Squish, squish, squash came a wet knocking on the door.

It was the big, bad wolf.

"Let me in, let me in," he growled.

"No, not by the hair of my chinny chin chin," squealed the pig.

"Then I'll huff and I'll puff and I'll blow your house in," said the wolf.

But before the wolf could do anything, the house collapsed with a wet *plop*, and the little pig took off as fast as his little piggy legs could carry him.

The second little pig had just finished building
his house when the first little pig came running up.

"There's a wolf after me," he gasped.

"Did he huff and puff and blow your house in?"
asked the second little pig.

"He didn't have time. Someone spilt juice on my house and it fell down all by itself," said the first pig.

"Well, it looks like he's coming to finish the job here," said the

second little pig. The wolf was almost at the house! They slammed the door just in time.

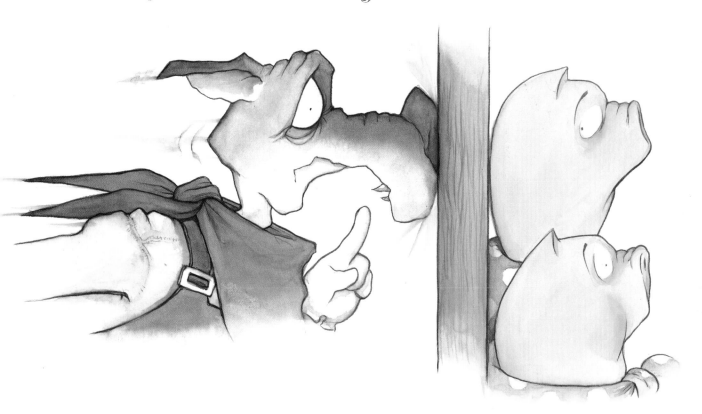

"OOOOOOWW!" howled the wolf. The door had slammed right in his face. But he was still hungry. "Yemt me yin, yemt me yin . . ." he began, clutching his nose. "Or I'll yuff and I'll nuff and . . ."

"Wait. I've got to redo the nose," interrupted a Voice from nowhere in particular.

While the wolf was getting his nose fixed,
the two little pigs ran out the back door.

The third little pig was enjoying a good book and a glass of pink lemonade when the two little pigs burst through his front door.

They told him about the spilt juice, the wolf with the hurt nose, and the mysterious Voice.

The third little pig jumped up and bolted the door.

"I know who the Voice is," he said, turning white as a ghost. "It's the ILLUSTRATOR."

"Yes, it's me. I'm the one who is painting this story," said the Voice, who was indeed the Illustrator. "And I'm sorry to tell you, but I just ran out of red paint. Without it, I can't make you pink. That's why you've all turned pale."

The first pig felt so faint he had to sit down.

The third little pig was
not happy.

"This is embarrassing,"
he said. "We have to be
some sort of color."

Suddenly the three little pigs felt queasy, like they were riding a boat on stormy seas.

They looked at one another and gasped. They were green. Green all over.

"Green? You made us *green?*" cried the third little pig.

"You don't like it?" said the Illustrator.

The three little pigs shook their green heads.

"Well, I'll try to think of something else. But be careful," the Illustrator continued. "The wolf's coming."

The wolf was, in fact, right at the door.

"Let me in, let me in!" he howled. All this running around was making him hungry. He didn't care what color the pigs were as long as he could gobble them up.

"No, not by the green hair of our green chinny chin chins," said the pigs.

"Well, then I'll huff,

and I'll puff,

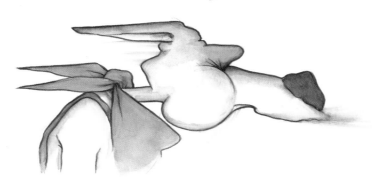

and I'll–"

"How's this?" interrupted the Illustrator.

The wolf peeked through the window and howled with laughter. The Illustrator had made the third little pig patterned!

"This is *not* funny," said the third little pig to the Illustrator. "Now I'm blending into the furniture!"

"You see?" he said when the first pig sat on him.

"I'm starting to feel like a real clown!"

Suddenly the third little pig *looked* like a clown. "Uh-oh," said the first little pig. "I think the Illustrator misunderstood you."

The second little pig explained to the Illustrator that the third little pig had said he *felt* like a clown, not that he wanted to *look* like one.

"Oops," said the Illustrator, and he made the third little pig pale again.

On the other side of the door, the wolf was still hungry. So he huffed and he puffed some more. But he just couldn't blow the house in.

So he decided
to climb down the
chimney instead.

The three little pigs heard the wolf on the roof.
"Quick, let's build a fire," said the third little pig.
"That'll keep him out."

They put more and more wood on the fire so it would get red hot and . . .

"Wait! No paint!" said the second little pig. "No red paint!"

No red paint meant no fire. No fire meant . . . the wolf would come down the chimney and gobble them up.

"Look!" shouted the third little pig to the Illustrator. "Because you ran out of red paint, the wolf is about to eat us up. Do something quick!

"WE DON'T WANT TO BE
IN THIS STORY ANYMORE!"

Once upon a time there were three bears—
a mama bear, a papa bear, and a little baby bear.